MARTHA BLAH BLAH

Susan Meddaugh

HOUGHTON MIFFLIN COMPANY BOSTON

For three Js, one D, and Cisco

Walter Lorraine *wl* Books

Library of Congress Cataloging-in-Publication Data

Meddaugh, Susan.

   Martha blah blah / Susan Meddaugh.

      p. cm.

   Summary: When the current owner of the soup company breaks the
founder's promise to have every letter of the alphabet in every can
of soup, Martha, the talking dog, takes action.

   ISBN 0-395-79755-1 (hardcover)

   [1. Dogs—Fiction.   2. Soups—Fiction.]   I. Title.

[E]—dc20   95-53275
                                                                    CIP
                                                                    AC

For information about this and other Houghton Mifflin trade
and reference books and multimedia products, visit The
Bookstore at Houghton Mifflin on the World Wide Web at
http://www.hmco.com/trade/.

Printed in the United States of America

WOZ   10 9 8 7 6 5 4 3

Martha was always a great communicator.

Sad ↑   Happy ↑   Mad ↑

But when she ate alphabet soup, the letters went up to her brain instead of down to her stomach,

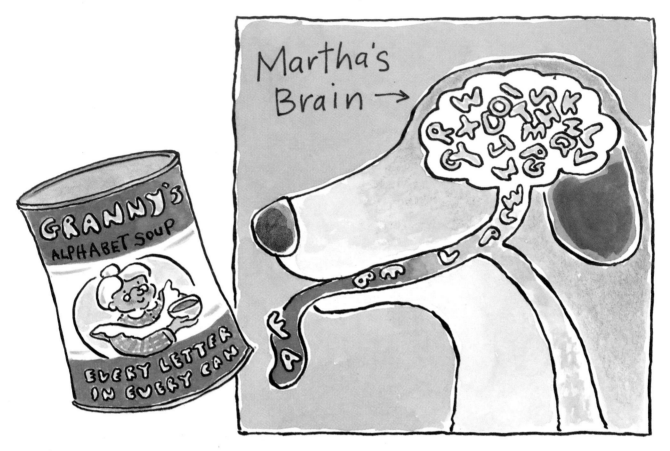

and Martha spoke words.

Isn't it time for my dinner?

Martha loved letters. She loved words.

So Martha's family gave her a bowl of alphabet soup every day.
Martha never missed a meal.

Having words opened up a world of possibilities for Martha.
All the employees at the local Burger Boy knew her well...

and the neighborhood dogs
depended on her.

Of course, Martha couldn't help but notice how much her family enjoyed having a talking dog. How special they thought she was.

There was someone else who loved letters as much as Martha. Alf Abbott was the A man at Granny's Soup Company. He made all the A's that went into alphabet soup.

Alf loved his job, and he was good at it. He assumed he would always have it.

Unfortunately, the new owner of Granny's Soup Company, Granny Flo, had other ideas. Granny Flo was looking at a portrait of the founder, Granny Elsie, when she made an important business decision.

But she was really thinking, "Fewer letters mean bigger profits."
So Granny Flo summoned her twenty-six alphabeticians and began to
draw letters from a hat. Thirteen alphabeticians were suddenly out of
work. One of them was Alf.

Within a week, cartons of the new soup went out to local supermarkets.
"No one will even notice the difference," thought Granny Flo.

But several days later, after finishing
her daily bowl of alphabet soup,
Martha said,

"What did you say?" asked Helen.

Helen giggled.
"How embarrassing!" thought Martha. "Must be a touch of
laryngitis."

* Good soup today.   ** I said: Good soup!

But it wasn't laryngitis. Strange sounds continued to come from Martha's mouth all day.

The next day wasn't any better.

* Hello. Gus has a short message.
** I'd like ten burgers. BURGERS! BURGERS!

Martha ate bowl after bowl of alphabet soup, but it was no use. Nothing she said made any sense at all.
"I'm afraid Martha is losing her ability to speak," said Helen's mother.

* No good.

"Oh no!" thought Martha. She couldn't imagine not being able to talk. No more Burger Boy? No more telephone calls? Just another dog, scratching on the door to go out.

And what would her family think if Martha lost her letters?

"I couldn't stand that," thought Martha, and she went outside.
She walked down the street, away from home, mumbling to
herself.

* My words are gone.   ** Where did they go?   *** What to do?

Martha had wandered for several hours when a familiar aroma reminded her that she had missed something important.

She followed her nose…

and her nose led her directly to Alf Abbott's kitchen,
where Alf was heating up a can of soup.
"Come in," said Alf, who missed his friends from the soup
company. He poured Martha a big bowl of alphabet soup.

Martha ate her soup happily, but without expectations, while Alf just gazed at the bowl in his lap.
"There it is!" he said. "A perfect A. And look at that L. Boy, Lou sure had a way with pasta."

Alf continued to admire each letter in his soup until Martha was almost asleep, lulled by the sweet sound of vowels and consonants. Then Alf said in the saddest voice, "My last can of *real* alphabet soup. It's just not the same since Granny left out half the letters."

The words came out of Martha's mouth perfectly clearly.

Martha didn't know whether to laugh or growl. To Alf's absolute astonishment, she started to sing.

♪ A B C D E F G ♫
H I J K L M N O P ♪
Q R S T U V W X Y and Z
Now I have all 26,
there are Soup
Cans to be fixed!
♫

Then she said,

Martha found Granny Flo
in her office.

She got right to the point.

Granny Flo turned angrily in her chair,
but all she could see was Granny Elsie, looking right at her.
Granny Flo was terrified!
"Did you speak?" she asked the portrait in a small voice.

"Every letter in every can," said Martha from behind the desk. "You promised!"

"But it was good for business," said Granny Flo to the portrait.

"Good *soup* is your business," said Martha.

Put all the letters back in the soup!

Granny Flo made the first of thirteen calls from beneath her desk. She began with A, of course.

Hello, Alf?

Martha was feeling better in every way when suddenly she heard familiar voices calling her name. Then her whole family was hugging her and talking at the same time. They were saying wonderful things…

and all before Martha could say even a word.